The Koala Who Bounced

Jimmy Thomson

Illustrated by Eric Löbbecke

RANDOM HOUSE AUSTRALIA

Karri the koala knew he was different when he fell off his mum's back . . . and bounced.

The Koala Who Bounced

Our thanks to Selwa Anthony
for making it happen. J&E

A Random House book
Published by Random House Australia Pty Ltd
Level 3, 100 Pacific Highway, North Sydney NSW 2060
www.randomhouse.com.au

First published by Random House Australia in 1993
This edition published by Random House Australia 2011

Addresses for companies within the Random House Group can be found at www.randomhouse.com.au/offices.

National Library of Australia
Cataloguing-in-Publication Entry

Author: Thomson, Jimmy
Title: The koala who bounced / Jimmy Thomson; illustrator Eric Löbbecke
ISBN: 978 1 74275 224 2
Dewey number: A823.3

Cover and internal design by Anna Warren, Warren Ventures
Typeset in 20/28 pt Berkeley Oldstyle Medium by Anna Warren, Warren Ventures
Printed and bound by Midas Printing

10 9 8 7 6 5 4 3 2 1

Yes, Karri could bounce through the air, chasing blowflies, bugs and dragonflies. The other young koalas tried to copy him but they got hurt.
And whenever Karri wanted to play, their mothers took them away and told him to stop bouncing.

Still, Karri was happy . . . until the day some workers came with machines and dogs. The other koalas rustled and bustled and scurried away. But Karri could bounce fast and far, and he left everyone behind.

Karri was lonely and scared. When the workers had gone, he went back to his old tree and found a message from his mum, in sniffs and nibbles, on a big gum leaf.

'Dear Karri,' she said, 'we're moving to somewhere safer. Remember to keep your eyes open, keep your ears clean and keep your nose sniffing and you'll be fine. Try to find us. I'm leaving you these directions to help you . . .'

But before Karri could read any more, a tear plopped onto the leaf and washed the message away.

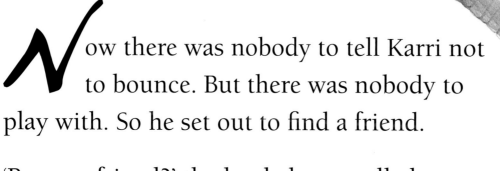

Now there was nobody to tell Karri not to bounce. But there was nobody to play with. So he set out to find a friend.

'Be your friend?' the kookaburra called. 'Don't make me laugh!' And he did!

The possum was too sleepy. The emu was too tall. The wallaby bounced too fast and the wise old wombat was TOO old. 'Try the platypus,' he said. 'She lives near a log by a bend in the river . . .'

'*I* don't suppose you can swim?' said the platypus. 'Koala paddle? Hmm? Go on . . . pop into the water!'

Karri just blinked.

'I thought not!' the platypus said rudely. 'Get lost, then! You're not even a real koala. Koalas don't bounce!'

There was a plop in the water where she had just been. Then there was another, and another, as the river swallowed up Karri's tears.

One day, when he was looking for his mum, Karri found a place full of people having fun. One of them was playing alone with . . . another bouncing koala!

Karri waited until it got dark. All the people went away, and left the other koala alone.

Karri looked closely. It didn't look much like a koala. He listened but it didn't say anything. He sniffed. It didn't smell like a koala. Karri prodded it but it just rolled away. Karri sighed. He wished his new friend wasn't so shy.

The next day the girl came and picked up the other bouncing koala. The she looked around, ran to the fence and slipped through. A little boy shouted, 'Kit! Come back!' But Kit kept running. 'It's no use,' the boy said. 'She can't hear.'

arri followed Kit until they came to lots of people playing with . . . ANOTHER bouncing koala!

Karri was a bit scared so he scrambled up a tree. Kit was down below, copying the players, but when she threw her koala up high, it landed right beside Karri.

Kit didn't see Karri until she had climbed onto the branch. Karri blinked. Kit blinked right back.

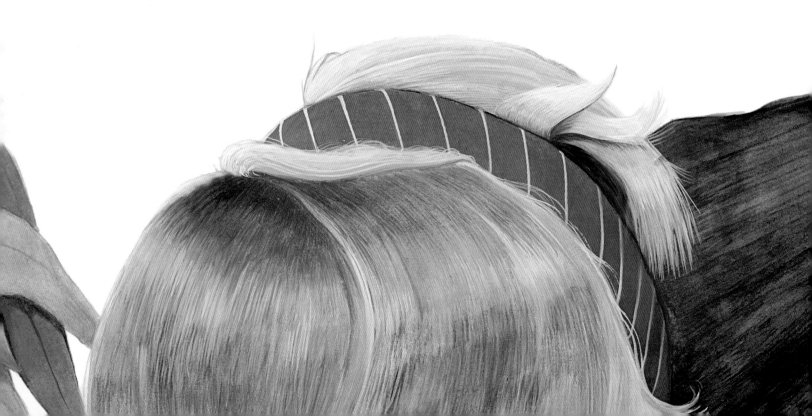

Karri said 'Hello' in koala. But Kit signalled that she couldn't hear or speak. So they just sat together happily to watch the game.

It was so exciting that Karri bounced high into the air. But when he sniffed he smelled . . . smoke!

He heard the cries of frightened children and saw a bushfire moving towards them. Some koalas were trapped too and one of them was his mum.

Kit couldn't warn the people down below but Karri could. He bounced out of the tree and in among the players as they tried to catch him.

*T*hen Karri bounced over to the tree, where Kit was pretending to be stuck, but the players thought she was really in trouble. Somebody shouted: 'Get a ladder!'

The man at the top of the ladder saw the smoke. 'FIRE! FIRE!' he shouted. 'There's a bushfire at the school!' And they rushed away to put it out.

*T*he fire was put out and everyone was safe. The koalas liked the children so much they decided to live in the trees nearby . . .

. . . and nobody ever again told
Karri not to bounce.